TEXT BY
Nikki Tate

ILLUSTRATIONS BY
Benoît Laverdière

Grandparents' Day

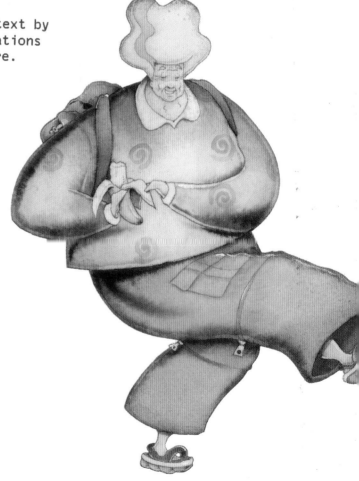

annick press
toronto + new york + vancouver

"Mom? Do I have to take Omi to Grandparents' Day?"
Mom whirls around so fast she knocks the bowl of peanuts
right off the coffee table. Peanuts skitter everywhere.

"Shh! What if Omi hears you!"
Mom doesn't understand that it's one thing to play games
and have fun with my strange grandmother at home, but it's
asking a lot to take her to school with me.

For starters, Omi looks weird. You can tell she doesn't believe in hairdressers. She cuts her own hair and washes it with soap instead of shampoo. Her favorite shoes are a pair of old green rubber boots held together with duct tape.

Omi doesn't even live in a house like normal
people. She lives on her boat and never
has the same address two weeks in a row.
She collects dead bugs from every continent
as a hobby.

"Ready?" Omi saunters into the living room. I look at her feet. Sensible sandals. That's a relief. Omi smiles at me. At least she's not a cheek-tweaker like Emily's grandmother.

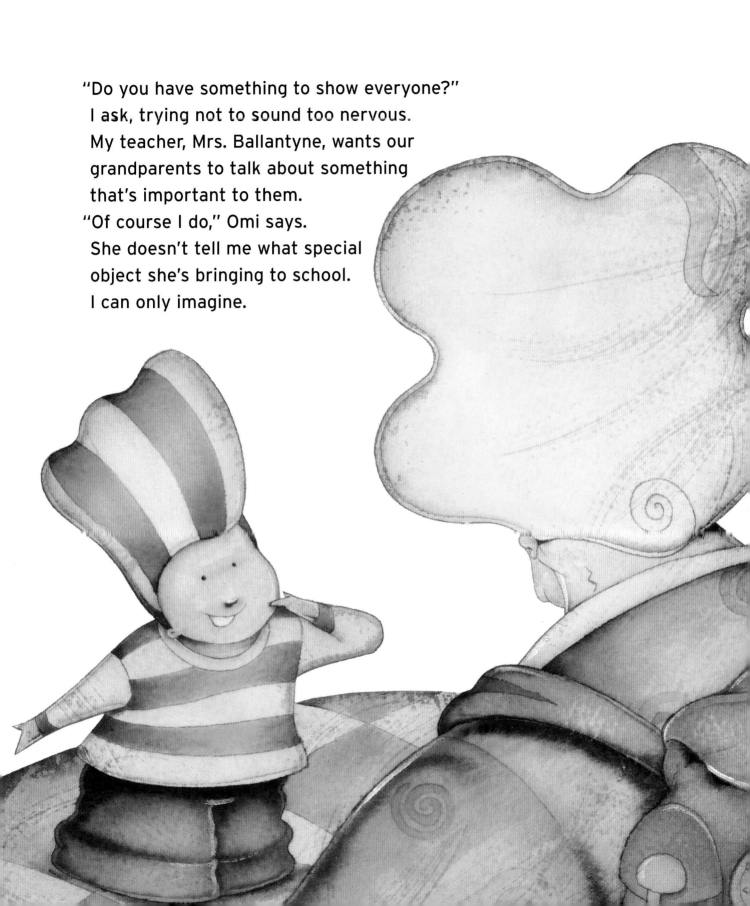

"Do you have something to show everyone?"
I ask, trying not to sound too nervous.
My teacher, Mrs. Ballantyne, wants our
grandparents to talk about something
that's important to them.
"Of course I do," Omi says.
She doesn't tell me what special
object she's bringing to school.
I can only imagine.

Mrs. Ballantyne's classroom looks very small with all those grandparents squished inside. Chairs scrape across the floor as the old people try to get comfortable.
Only Mr. Elliot looks at home. He's sitting in his wheelchair with his feet up. When Adam introduces him he says:

"This is my Great-grandpa Elliot. I had to bring him because
my one grandpa's dead, the other one lives in Milwaukee,
and both my grandmas live in Florida."

"Thank you, Adam." Mrs. Ballantyne squints at the clock. "Next?"
One by one all the kids say something about their grandparents.

When it's my turn I just say, "This is my Omi. That's German for grandmother." They don't need to know anything else.

The knot in my stomach tightens a little when Mrs. Ballantyne says, "Did everyone remember to bring something to talk about?" I still don't know what Omi has in mind.

Mrs. Lim shows us photographs of herself teaching a fitness class for pregnant ladies. They do exercises right in the swimming pool at the community center! She makes us all stand up and stretch and tells us how important it is to drink lots of water every day.

Jocelyn's grandma shows us 22 tiny dolls from different countries.
She won't let us touch them, though. But that's okay—we understand
just how precious they are.

Mr. Elliot has brought a dusty old book about Sherlock Holmes. "I've been operating Whodunnit Books for 37 years," he says, and gives us each a business card to take home to show our parents.

Then, it's Omi's turn. I watch to see what
she's going to pull out of her backpack —
camel bells, maybe — or a shark's tooth.
But she doesn't even look at her backpack.

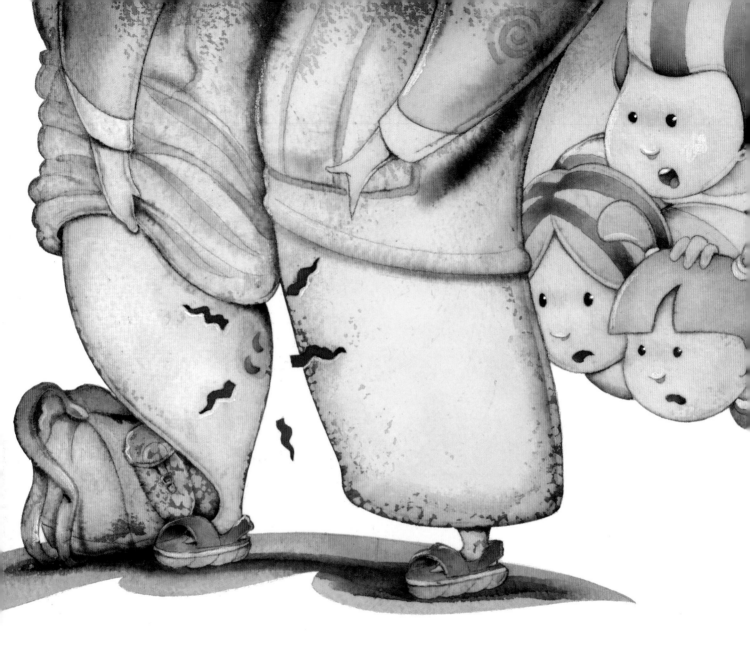

My grandmother, in front of everyone, leans forward and slowly
pulls up her pant leg. Everyone can see her sensible sandal.
She tugs her pant leg higher until we are all staring at her calf.
Everyone gasps at the huge, purplish blue-black scar on the
back of her leg. It looks as if someone has dug out a hollow and
then painted it — not very neatly, either.

"Wow! What happened?" Jacob asks.

"Snakebite," Omi says, and Ellen covers her eyes with her hands.
Even Mr. Thornton, who fought in a war, goes pale.

"It happened in Brazil many years ago. I was much younger—
not much more than a child myself."

Toby and Alicia lean forward, eyes wide, mouths open.

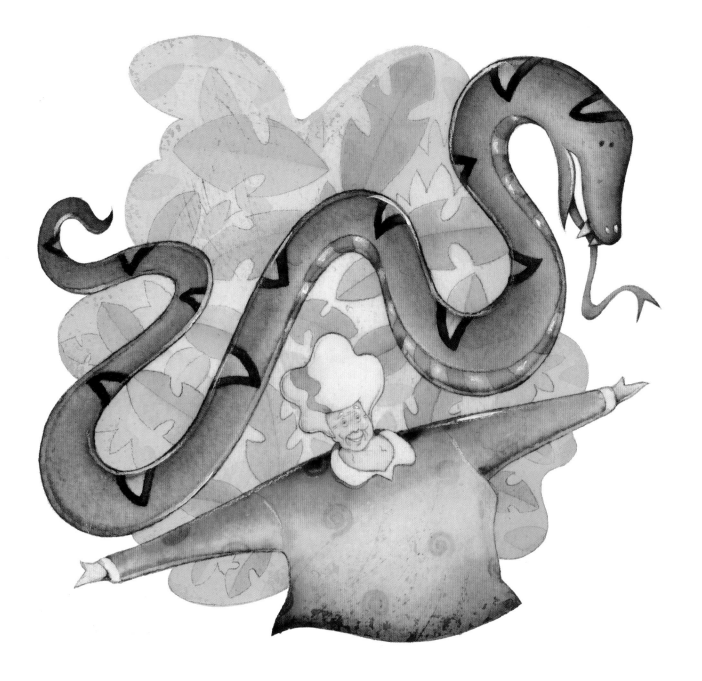

"The snake was huge—" she pulls her hands apart to show us how
 big it was, "it was green and brown with stripes across its back and
 black and gold eyes."
"Where was it?" Alicia asks, leaning so far forward she nearly falls
 off her chair.

"At first it was under a log, which is why I didn't see it right away. But I sure saw it when it struck. **Whap!**" She smacks her open palm against her calf and we all jump back, hearts thudding. "That snake sank its fangs into my leg."

"Eeeewwwwww!" Chandra says with a shudder.
"What did you do?" Mrs. Lim asks, her bottled water trembling
in her hands.

Omi opens her mouth and screams and a bunch of the kids scream right along with her. I nearly leap out of my skin. Even Mrs. Ballantyne squeaks. I'm pretty sure Grandparents' Day has never been this exciting before.

I look behind me as if a snake might be hiding, ready to jump out and bite me. Chandra lifts her feet and wraps them around the legs of her stool.
"I was miles from home in the jungle. I had to save myself...
I pulled out my knife."

Omi's hand flashes this way and that, showing how she sliced at the wound to make it bleed. "Then I sucked out the poison and spat it on the ground. *Pfit. Pfit.*"

"Amazing!"

"Can I touch it?"

Poor Mrs. Ballantyne. Everybody wants to hear more of Omi's stories. Nobody is very interested in the wooden duck Mr. Sherez carved and painted himself, even though he's polished the wings so much they practically glow.

When the last of the grandparents has spoken, it's hard to get close to Omi because everybody wants to talk to her. Toby asks for Omi's autograph. Omi laughs her deep, rolling laugh and signs his math book.

After snacktime, Omi takes my hand and squeezes it. When she starts talking about the time she was stranded on an island without fresh water, everyone falls silent to hear what happened.

"Did you know there is fresh water in fish eyeballs?"
Mrs. Ballantyne gasps.
"Luckily for the fish, I found a muddy puddle to drink from."
"Oh yuck!" I say, squirming. But it's a giggly, exciting kind of
squirm and I sort of like it.
"Some cures," Omi says, "are much worse than the disease."
"Let's get started on our friendship bracelets, shall we?"
Mrs. Ballantyne says before Omi can give us any
more examples.

At lunchtime, Mrs. Ballantyne shoos everyone out of the classroom and as I walk home with Omi I tell her, "I hope nobody ever finds a cure for weirdness."

She raises her eyebrows and says, "I don't know anybody weird, do you?"

"Me either," I say. "But if I did, I wouldn't want them to change."

And right there in the middle of the sidewalk Omi stops.

She reaches into her pocket and pulls out a small compass. "I was going to tell them about the time I got lost in the Tateyama Mountains in Japan. This compass saved my life." Omi winks and places the compass in the palm of my hand. "You might need this," she says, smiling, "to get you out of trouble some day."

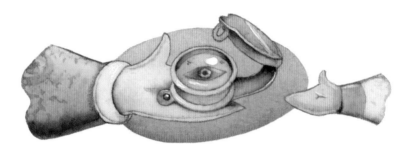

Omi shows me which direction to travel and then, holding my new compass in front of me, I lead the way home.

Annick Press Ltd.

We acknowledge the support of the Canada Council for the Arts, the Ontario Arts Council, and the Government of Canada through the Book Publishing Industry Development Program (BPIDP) for our publishing activities.

Copy editing by Elizabeth McLean
Cover design and interior design by Irvin Cheung/iCheung Design
The text was typeset in Interstate
The art was rendered in watercolor with mixed media

Cataloging in Publication
Tate, Nikki, 1962-
    Grandparents' Day / Nikki Tate ; illustrated by Benoît Laverdière.

For children ages 5-8.
ISBN 1-55037-843-0 (bound).–ISBN 1-55037-842-2 (pbk.)

    I. Laverdière, B. (Benoît) II. Title.

PS8589.A8735G73 2004   jC813'.54   C2004-901083-2

Printed and bound in China.

Published in the U.S.A. by	**Distributed in Canada by**	**Distributed in the U.S.A. by**
Annick Press (U.S.) Ltd.	Firefly Books Ltd.	Firefly Books (U.S.) Inc.
	66 Leek Crescent	P.O. Box 1338
	Richmond Hill, ON	Ellicott Station
	L4B 1H1	Buffalo, NY 14205

Visit our website at: **www.annickpress.com**

For Mom and for Omi – I could not have chosen better ancestors.

                    –N.T.

Merci à Cécile qui a su me soutenir tout au long de ce travail et qui m'a inspiré cet agréable personnage de grand-mère.

                    –B.L.